Disney
101 DALMATIANS

*This is the story of two brave Dalmatians, ninety-nine puppies,
and one of the greatest rescues of all time.*

Printed in the U.S.A. • ISBN: 1-40372-340-0
15180 Disney Flip Over Storybook – Disney's 101 Dalmatians and Lady and the Tramp
06 07 08 09 NGS 10 9 8 7 6 5 4 3 2 1

Roger Radcliffe was a musician. He lived in an apartment in London with Pongo, his pet Dalmatian dog.

One splendid day, Roger got married. His lovely new wife was named Anita—and she had a beautiful lady Dalmatian named Perdita. Pongo and Perdita fell in love, too.

Soon, Perdita and Pongo became the proud parents of fifteen little puppies.

Life seemed perfect... until an old friend of Anita's—Cruella De Vil!—came to see the puppies.

"Where are the puppies?" Cruella said. "I just *adore* Dalmatian puppies! Their coats are so beautiful. I'll buy all of them!"

"Oh, no, you won't," said Roger. "They're *not* for sale."

"You fools!" Cruella cried. "You'll be sorry!" And she stormed out of the house.

One night, Cruella sent her two henchmen, the Badun Brothers, to dognap the puppies!

The police immediately launched an investigation, but as the days went by, the puppies were still not found.

At last, Pongo said to Perdita, "The humans aren't getting anywhere. We'll have to find the puppies ourselves."

Pongo decided to try the Twilight Bark. This was the quickest way for dogs to send and receive news across the country.

That evening, from the top of Primrose Hill, Pongo
sent the alarm:

"Bark, bark, bark, h-o-w-l!"

Then Pongo and Perdita waited.

After a moment, an answering bark was heard.

"It's the Great Dane at Hampstead!" said Pongo,
and he barked the message about the missing puppies.

Danny the Great Dane was very surprised by the message. "Fifteen Dalmatian puppies have been stolen!" he told a terrier friend. "It's up to us to send out an all-dog alert with the Twilight Bark."

Danny's big, deep voice began to send the news all over London.

Two dogs heard the alert and spread the news. Then two more. Within the hour, word was spreading all over England.

Before too long, the Twilight Bark reached an old sheepdog called the Colonel, who lived on a farm.

The Colonel's friends—a horse named the Captain and a cat named Sergeant Tibs—listened too. They were all concerned to hear that fifteen puppies had been stolen.

"That's funny," Tibs said to the Captain and the Colonel. "I heard puppies barking over at the old De Vil house last night."

"But no one lives there now," said the Colonel. "We must go and see what's going on."

So the Colonel and Tibs went quietly up to the house and peered through a broken window.

Inside the house, Horace and Jasper Badun were eating supper and relaxing in front of the television.

All around the room there were puppies.
Not fifteen puppies.
Not even fifty puppies.
Tibs counted *ninety-nine* puppies!

The Colonel quickly returned to the Captain's stable and loudly barked the good news. Within no time at all, the Twilight Bark sent the message all the way back to London that the puppies had been found.

The good news finally reached the ears of Perdita and Pongo. They set off across the snowy countryside as fast as they could to rescue their puppies.

Meanwhile, Sergeant Tibs was keeping watch on the house. When he saw Cruella drive up to the front door, he went to the broken window to hear what was happening.

Cruella was barking out orders. "I want their skins for fur coats!" she cried. "I'll be back first thing in the morning." And with that warning, she left.

Fur coats!

How awful!

Tibs could not believe it.

He had to save these poor puppies!

There wasn't a moment to lose. As soon as the Baduns began watching television again, Tibs crept through the broken window and whispered to the nearest puppy, "Tell everyone they must escape. Cruella is after your coats!"

When all the puppies had been alerted, Tibs led them out of the room and up the stairs to find a hiding place.

As soon as the Baduns discovered that the puppies were gone, they searched all over the house and eventually headed up the stairs…

...and there were the puppies, cowering in a corner of the bedroom, with Tibs in front, ready to protect them from the Baduns!

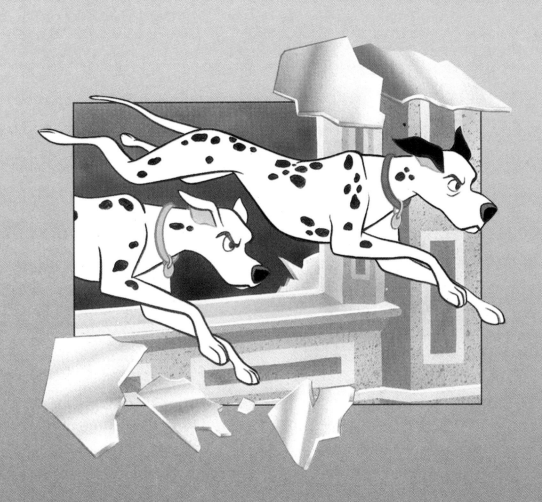

Meanwhile, the Colonel had met up with Perdita and Pongo and led them to the De Vil house. They arrived just in the nick of time and quickly bounded into action.

Perdita went after Horace, while Pongo tore at Jasper Badun's trousers.

As the fight was going on, Sergeant Tibs led the puppies out of the house to the safety of the Captain's stable.

Leaving the Baduns in a heap on the floor, Perdita and Pongo dashed after the puppies.

"Are our fifteen all here?" asked Perdita anxiously.

"Your fifteen and a few more," replied the Captain. "There are *ninety-nine!*"

"*Ninety-nine!*" said Pongo, astonished. "Whatever did Cruella want with *ninety-nine* puppies?"

There was silence for a moment, then one little puppy said, "She was going to make fur coats out of us."

Perdita and Pongo looked at each other in horror. They had never heard of anything so evil.

"We'll just have to take them *all* back to London with us," said Perdita. "I'm sure Roger and Anita will look after them."

Perdita, Pongo, and the puppies set off back to London, leaving a trail of pawprints in the snow.

Cruella, who had returned for the puppies' coats, quickly spotted the pawprints—and the chase began....

Eventually, after trudging across the countryside, Perdita and Pongo led the tired puppies to the shelter of a black-smith's shop. Cruella and the Baduns were still on their trail.

Suddenly, Pongo had an idea. He made the puppies roll in some soot until they all looked like black Labradors.

"Quick! Into this van!" said Pongo. "It's going to London!"

As the van sped away, Cruella spotted the dogs.

"Hmmm…" she said, "I think I have been tricked! After them!"

Cruella caught up with the van and tried to sideswipe it with her car…

…but the van kept going; and Cruella and the Baduns ended their chase in a car crash.

"You fools!" cried Cruella, as the Dalmatians escaped to London.

Back in London and home at last, the tired, sooty puppies received warm hugs from Roger and Anita, who noticed that there seemed to be a lot more of them.

"Fourteen, fifteen," counted Roger, "sixty-two—ninety-four—and five over there. That's a hundred and one Dalmatians, counting Perdita and Pongo!"

"Whatever are we going to do with them all?" asked Anita.

"Why, keep them of course," said Roger. "We'll buy a big house and have a Dalmatian Plantation!"

"Aye," said Jock, smiling at each mischievous little pooch. "But there's a bit of their father in them, too!"

As it turned out, Jock had nothing to worry about. In fact, good old Trusty hobbled out to go visiting with Jock the very next Christmas. And the first place they visited was the home of their dear friends, Lady and Tramp.

That's right. Tramp had finally traded in his wandering ways for a collar and a home with his Lady. And now they had puppies: Scooter, Fluffy, Ruffy—and little Scamp, who looked just like his dad.

"They've got their mother's eyes," Trusty said.

Outside, Trusty and Jock heard about Tramp saving the baby and decided to go after the dogcatcher's wagon.

"We'll track 'em down," yelled Trusty as they ran.

"And then?" asked Jock.

"We'll hold 'em—hold 'em at bay!"

The brave Trusty followed Tramp's scent and chased down the wagon, but his barking scared the dogcatcher's horses. They reared up and tipped the wagon over, pinning Trusty under a wheel.

Jock began to howl. Would he ever talk with old Trusty again?

Just then, Jim Dear and Darling came home and Lady led them up to the baby's room to show them the dead rat. All at once, everyone understood. Tramp hadn't been trying to hurt the baby—he had saved it!

Was there time to stop the dogcatcher's wagon before Tramp ended up at the pound?

However, Aunt Sarah did not see the dead rat. She only saw two dogs and an overturned crib.

"You—you vicious brutes!" she screamed at Lady and Tramp. "Back! Get back!"

Aunt Sarah locked Lady in the cellar and called the dogcatcher to take Tramp away for attacking the baby.

Lady broke loose and ran into the baby's room, too, just in time to see the rat escape from Tramp and climb onto the baby's crib. But Tramp flew at the rat, saving the baby from harm.

Luckily, Tramp heard Lady barking. He raced into the yard and over to Lady.

"What's wrong, Pidge?" he asked.

"A rat!" cried Lady.

"Where?" asked Tramp.

"Upstairs. In the baby's room!"

Tramp raced up the back porch stairs and into the baby's room and attacked the rat. He knew it was up to him to protect the baby.

Lady was happy to be home again, but it didn't last long. Instead of allowing Lady inside, Aunt Sarah chained her to the doghouse!

Lady was heartbroken, and so lost in unhappy thoughts that she didn't see a huge rat climb into the backyard. But when it ran in front of her, she took off after him, barking and growling— only to be stopped short by her chain!

Watching the rat climb up the side of the house and through the baby's window, Lady grew desperate and barked with her whole heart.

Lady was ashamed and afraid—especially when the other dogs made fun of her. Luckily, a Pekingese dog named Peg came to her rescue.

"Can't ya see the poor kid's scared enough already?" Peg said. "They don't mean no real harm," she told Lady.

It was just that the other dogs were jealous. They knew that with the license on her collar, Lady would be released from the pound shortly.

And, sure enough, a guard soon came for Lady. "You're too nice a girl to be in this place," he said, handing Lady to Aunt Sarah.

The next morning, however, Lady realized she should be home, and Tramp agreed to take her back.

On the way, Tramp spotted a chicken coop.

"Ever chase chickens, Pidge?" Tramp asked.

"I should say not," Lady replied.

"Then you have never lived!" said Tramp, showing her how to crawl under the fence to the henhouse.

They sent the chickens squawking and squealing, but Lady hated every minute of it, especially when the farmer began to chase them.

Tramp scrambled through a hole under the fence but Lady was caught and taken to the pound!

...they kissed!

Nose to nose, staring deeply into each other's eyes, Lady and Tramp fell head over paws in love.

After their romantic dinner, the two dogs walked to the top of a hill. Above them they saw the twinkling stars in the sky. In all this beauty, Lady forgot about Aunt Sarah and her cats. She felt happy and in love.

Then Tony set the table, put down the spaghetti, and began to serenade the happy couple.

The two dogs shared a delicious spaghetti dinner by candlelight. As they ate, Tramp nibbled one end of a noodle, and Lady nibbled the other end of the same noodle. They nibbled and nibbled that noodle, until…

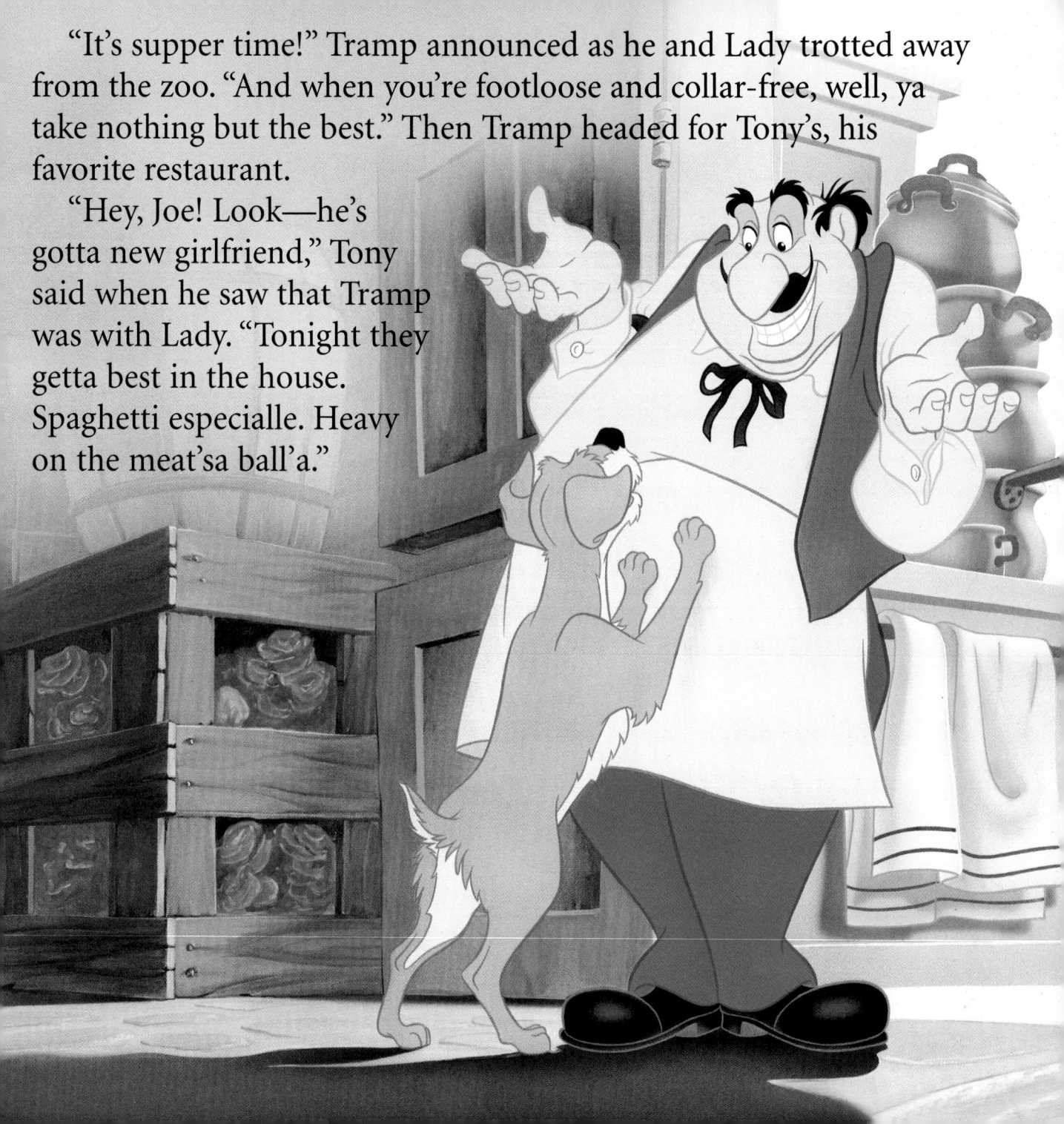

"It's supper time!" Tramp announced as he and Lady trotted away from the zoo. "And when you're footloose and collar-free, well, ya take nothing but the best." Then Tramp headed for Tony's, his favorite restaurant.

"Hey, Joe! Look—he's gotta new girlfriend," Tony said when he saw that Tramp was with Lady. "Tonight they getta best in the house. Spaghetti especialle. Heavy on the meat'sa ball'a."

Tramp took Lady to the zoo to see a beaver who was hauling trees to the swamp.

"What you need is a handy-dandy log puller," said Tramp to the beaver, pointing to the muzzle on Lady's face.

"Mind if I slip it on for size?" the beaver asked.

"Help yourself, friend," said Tramp, with a wink.

So the happy beaver carefully bit through the strap—and tried it on.

"It's off!" cried Lady happily.

She and Tramp went on their way.

Suddenly, a pack of dogs began chasing Lady!
Tramp happened to be passing by and saw that Lady was in trouble. He bared his teeth and growled at the other dogs, chasing them away.

"Ya poor kid," Tramp said, looking at Lady's muzzle. "We've gotta get this off. And I think I know the very place. Come on."

"I want a good strong muzzle," Aunt Sarah told the pet store clerk.

Lady wasn't sure what a muzzle was, but when the clerk strapped one on her, she suddenly understood. It was a terrible thing! Lady twisted and turned, struggling wildly, and then got loose and ran off down the street.

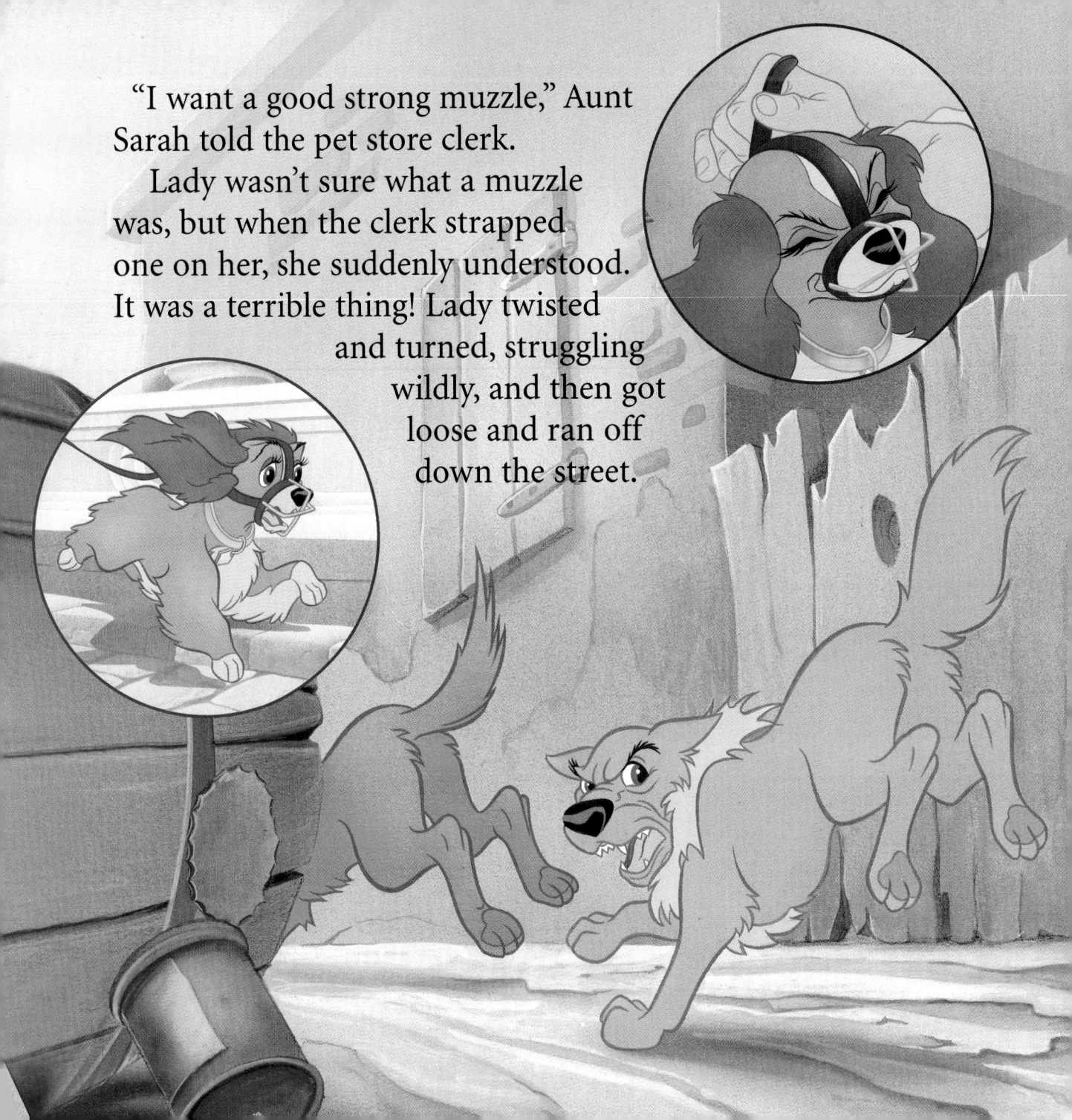

Crash! Bang! The cats wrecked the whole living room!

Hearing the noise, Aunt Sarah came flying downstairs. She took one look at Lady and screamed:

"Oh, merciful heavens! You wicked animal! Attacking my poor innocent little angels."

Then she scooped up Lady and marched off to the pet store.

For a while, things were wonderful. But one day Aunt Sarah came to stay at the house while Jim Dear and Darling went on a trip. As soon as they left, Aunt Sarah spotted Lady in the baby's room and yelled, "Get out of here!"

But even worse than Aunt Sarah were her naughty Siamese cats—out to cause nothing but trouble. They leaped at the birdcage, broke a vase, scratched the piano—and pulled the fishbowl off the table!

One day soon after, the baby arrived. And when Lady got a glimpse of him, she had to admit this thing called a baby was very cute. There was no sense in listening to that awful Tramp.

"Your humans are having a baby, a cute little bundle of trouble," Tramp said, swaggering over. "Remember that nice, warm bed by the fire? Get ready for a leaky doghouse, Pigeon. The dog moves out when the baby moves in!"

"Dinna listen, lassie," Jock said to Lady. Jock didn't trust a mutt like Tramp.

Tramp had the freedom to wander far and wide, and one day he overheard Lady telling her friends her troubles.

"Everyone is acting so strangely," she said. "Jim Dear rushes by without patting me on the head, and Darling hasn't taken me for a walk in ages. All they talk about is a 'happy event.'"

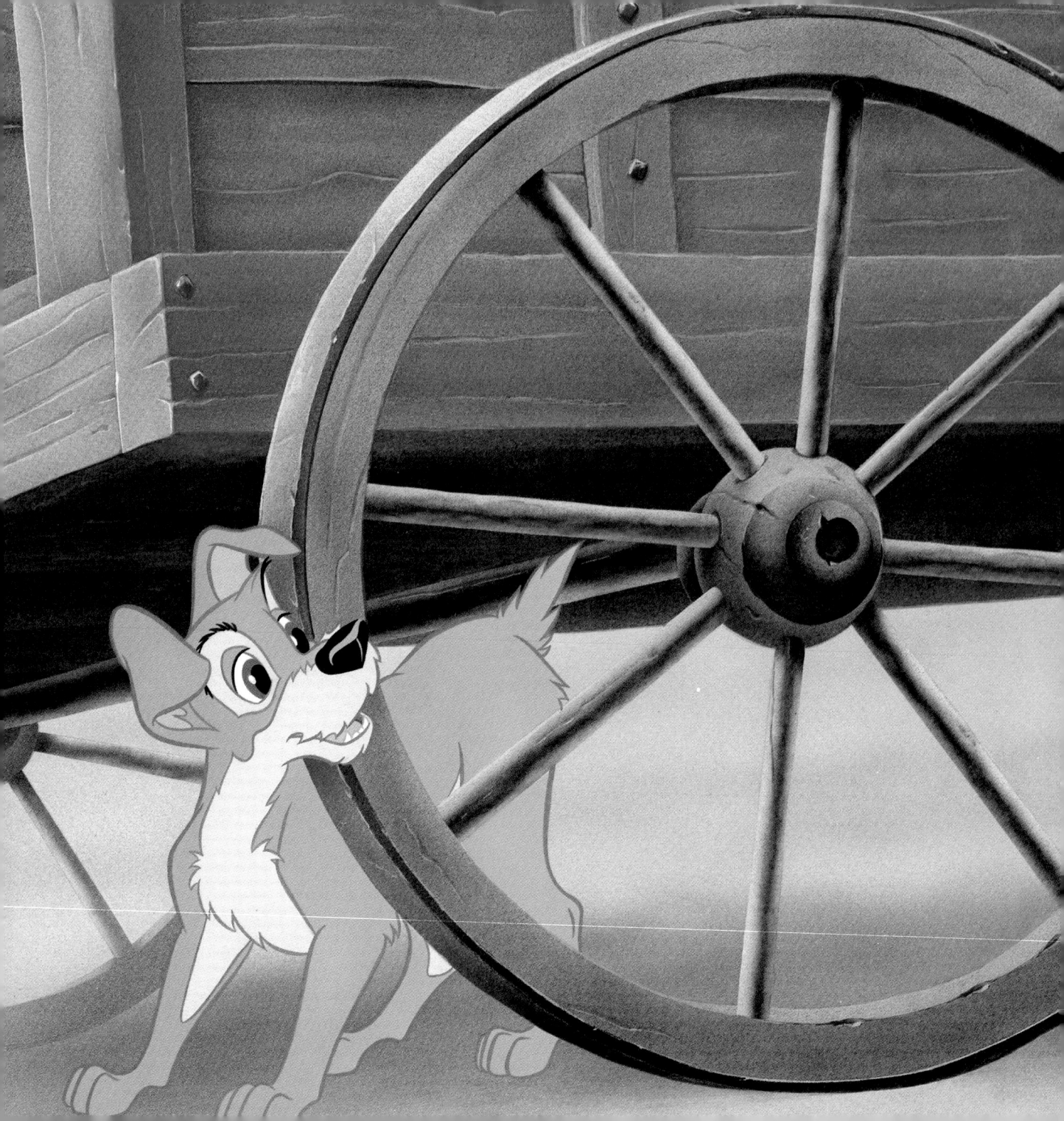

But some dogs didn't get to live in nice houses and wear new collars. They lived on the streets. The dogcatcher was always hunting them down in his wagon.

These dogs had one friend they knew they could count on—a mutt named Tramp. He was such a clever fellow, he never got caught. And he helped the others escape if they were nabbed by the dogcatcher.

When Lady was six months old, she received her very own collar with a special license engraved with her name. Now she knew she really belonged. Proudly, Lady showed it off to her neighbors, a Scottish terrier named Jock and a bloodhound named Trusty.

"Why, Miss Lady," exclaimed Trusty, "you have a collar!"

"Aye," Jock added, "she's a full-grown lady now."

Jim Dear and Darling loved Lady.
They were always petting and pampering her.
And, in return, Lady watched over the house.

It was Christmas Eve!

At the home of Jim Dear and Darling, many brightly wrapped presents sat under the tree. But one was particularly cheery. Jim Dear picked it out first and handed it to his bride, saying, "This is for you, Darling."

And as Darling lifted the lid off the box, out jumped a cuddly cocker spaniel puppy.

"Oh, how sweet!" cried Darling. "She's a perfectly beautiful little lady."

And so "Lady" became the puppy's name.

WALT DISNEY'S

Lady and the TRAMP

*This is the story of a lovely Lady and a rascally
Tramp whose hearts are bound by loyalty and love.*